Usicka

(416)
746-2865
or (416)
748-3666

MARY-KATE & ASHLEY

Starring in

winning london ™

P9-DEM-611

A novelization by Elizabeth J. Kruger

Based on the teleplay by
Karol Ann Hoeffner

HarperEntertainment
An Imprint of HarperCollins*Publishers*

A PARACHUTE PRESS BOOK

PARACHUTE
PRESS

Parachute Publishing, L.L.C.
156 Fifth Avenue
New York, NY 10010

 DUALSTAR
PUBLICATIONS

Dualstar Publications
c/o Thorne and Company
1801 Century Park East
Los Angeles, CA 90067

HarperEntertainment

An Imprint of HarperCollins*Publishers*
10 East 53rd Street, New York, NY 10022.

Copyright © 2001 Dualstar Entertainment Group, Inc. All rights reserved.
All photography copyright © 2001 Dualstar Entertainment Group, Inc.
All rights reserved.

Book created and produced by Parachute Publishing, L.L.C., in cooperation with
Dualstar Publications, a division of Dualstar Entertainment Group, Inc., published by
HarperEntertainment, an imprint of HarperCollins Publishers.

If you purchased this book without a cover, you should be aware that this book is
stolen property. It was reported as "unsold and destroyed" to the publisher, and
neither the author nor the publisher has received payment for this "stripped book."

No part of this publication may be reproduced in whole or in part, or stored in a
retrieval system, or transmitted in any form or by any means, electronic, mechanical,
photocopying, recording, or otherwise, without written permission of the publisher.

For information, address HarperCollins Publishers Inc.
10 East 53rd Street, New York, NY 10022.

ISBN 0-06-106666-4

HarperCollins®, ■®, and HarperEntertainment™ are trademarks of
HarperCollins Publishers Inc.

First printing: May 2001

Printed in the United States of America

Visit HarperEntertainment on the World Wide Web at
www.harpercollins.com

10 9 8 7 6 5 4 3 2 1

CHAPTER ONE

"Slow down!" Riley Lawrence called as her horse pounded over the field. Her sister, Chloe, galloped ahead at top speed.

Chloe raced down a hill, way ahead of Riley. Riley winced as Chloe's horse tore straight through a huge puddle. Globs of mud sprayed up from the horse's hooves. "Ugh! What a mess," Riley muttered.

"Try to catch me!" Chloe called back over her shoulder. She urged her horse on. "Faster, boy, faster!"

Riley rolled her eyes. They were supposed to be exercising the horses for the stable owner. But everything with Chloe had to be a contest. *Why can't she just have fun?* Riley wondered. She tugged on her horse's reins. He swerved around the puddle and slowed to a trot.

Chloe was waiting for Riley at the stable gate, breathless and grinning.

"Why do you always turn everything into a

race?" Riley asked as she trotted up.

"I play to win," Chloe declared. She leaned over and patted her horse on the neck.

"Well, I play to play," Riley said.

"That's your problem," Chloe shot back.

Riley shook her head. It was useless to argue. *We may look similar,* she thought, gazing at Chloe's blond hair and big blue eyes. *But we're so different inside!*

The girls got off their horses and led them into the stables. They handed the reins to the stable owner, who gave them each some money for a job well done.

The sisters sat down on a bench to take off their riding boots. "So, are you coming to the Model UN competition tonight?" Chloe asked, tugging on her boot.

"No chance," Riley said. She could think of about a zillion other things she'd rather do.

"*Brian's* going to be there," Chloe said.

Brian? Riley's cheeks suddenly heated up. "No chance I'd miss it...is what I meant," she added quickly.

Brian Conners. The name was like a little bell that had been ringing in Riley's ear since the day she laid eyes on him. Six years ago he moved into the house next door to them. He was ten, she was eight. She'd had a huge crush on him ever since.

Brian's parents became close friends with Riley's parents. The Conners family was always around for special occasions—birthdays, anniversaries. They even took vacations together. Riley and Brian were good friends—until two years ago.

Then Brian went to high school, became star running back for Lakeview High's football team— and forgot all about Riley.

Now Brian was a junior, and Riley was a freshman at Lakeview High. Finally, she was back in his world.

But do I have a chance with him? she wondered.

There was only one way to find out.

"I'll be there tonight," Riley said, picturing Brian's wavy brown hair and incredibly blue eyes. "Definitely."

Chloe twirled her hair nervously as she reread her notes. The mood was tense backstage. This was the final round of the Regional Model United Nations Competition. And Chloe wanted to win.

Each participating school in the Model UN was given a country to study. Chloe's team had been assigned China. Tonight she would be asked some tough questions about world issues, and she had to know how China would answer them. She paced back and forth, going over facts and figures in her head.

Someone tapped her on the shoulder. Chloe whirled around and found herself staring into a camera lens. Dylan Travis, her tall and skinny Hawaiian-shirted teammate, adjusted the focus on his digital video camera. The DV cam was like his wallet—he never left home without it. Dylan was always filming everyone doing everything.

Chloe frowned at him. "Dylan, I'm trying to concentrate," she said.

"Work with me," Dylan told Chloe. "This will just take a minute." He zoomed in on her. "The pressure is on for Chloe Lawrence. It's up to this young warrior to lead her team to victory. Oh, the human drama of competition! The intense focus!" He burped, then added, "The chili dog I had for lunch...."

"Ew, that was really gross." Chloe made a funny face and put her hand over his camera lens. "Go away, please."

Chloe watched as Dylan spun his focus to Rachel Byrd, another one of their teammates. Rachel glanced up from her index cards. She pushed her auburn hair off her face. "Maybe we could do this some other time, Dylan," she said sweetly.

Rachel does everything sweetly, Chloe thought. *She doesn't have a mean bone in her body.*

Mr. Holmes, their debate coach, hurried toward them. He was a short, wiry man and was wearing a Lakeview High football jacket. "Okay, team, bring it in," he said, pulling them into a huddle. Mr. Holmes usually coached Lakeview's football team. Model UN was his off-season assignment.

Brian, Rachel, Dylan, and Chloe gathered around Mr. Holmes. Randall Treece, a skinny kid with braces and black horn-rimmed glasses, joined them.

"It's late in the fourth quarter," Mr. Holmes began. "We're at the fifteen yard line. Last play of the game. We need a touchdown. Not a first down. Not a field goal. Get my drift?"

Chloe grinned. Mr. Holmes's pep talks were a little strange, but she liked them.

"Next up, Lakeview High," an announcer called.

Chloe's heart thumped as she led her teammates onstage. The competition was about to begin!

CHAPTER TWO

"When is this going to *end*?" Riley mumbled as she watched Chloe give her speech. She slumped in her seat at the back of the auditorium and yawned. *Model UN is just not very exciting*, she thought. Social studies was her least favorite subject in school.

"In conclusion, it's important to protect the citizens of China from dangerous ideas," Chloe declared. She gazed out from behind the podium at the crowd of students that filled the auditorium. "Freedom of speech does more harm than good. Thank you." She nodded politely to the judges sitting in the front row of the audience, then stepped away from the microphone.

Brian Conners stepped up to the podium next. "On behalf of Lakeview High, thank you, Mr. Secretary General," he said.

Riley sat up quickly. "Whoo-hoo! Go, China!" she cheered enthusiastically. She turned to the red-haired girl sitting next to her. "Isn't he *fabulous*?"

The head judge, a balding man in a brown suit,

walked onto the stage carrying a clipboard. "Thanks to all. It's been a great competition." He placed his papers on the podium and cleared his throat. "And now, I'm pleased to announce that the winner, with three hundred seventy-five points, is…" He looked out at the audience. "France. Congratulations, Woodrow Wilson Academy!"

The Woodrow Wilson fans cheered and clapped.

"Uh-oh," Riley muttered as she saw Chloe's expression. Chloe did *not* look happy.

The judge held up his hands for quiet. "And finally, the winner of the Golden Dove Award for outstanding delegate is…Ms. Chloe Lawrence!"

Chloe went back onstage to collect her award from the judge. She was smiling, but Riley could tell that her sister still wasn't satisfied.

Well, at least she won something, Riley thought. *Anyway, it's just a dumb competition. What's the big deal?*

Riley headed out to the lobby, where the post-competition party was starting. She scanned the crowded room until she spotted Chloe, Dylan, and Rachel near the snack table. She pushed toward them.

Rachel was trying to comfort Chloe. "Come on, third place isn't the end of the world," Riley heard her say.

"Yeah, and you won that golden goose award," Dylan added, "and we all got these cool little trophies." He held the small gold globes up to his earlobes like earrings.

Riley smiled at the joke.

But Chloe didn't laugh. "Third place is no place," she muttered.

Rachel shrugged. "Come on, Dylan, let's get something to drink." They moved off into the crowd.

Riley tugged on her sister's hair. "Nice job."

"Thanks," Chloe mumbled, shrugging.

Riley tried again. "And congrats on that golden goose award."

"Golden *Dove*," Chloe replied.

"Oh. Right," Riley said. "At any rate, you won."

"Yes, but my team didn't."

Riley felt a twinge of annoyance. Why did Chloe have to be such a bad loser? Why couldn't she just lighten up? Have some fun? "Well, I'm going to mingle. See you."

Riley moved away. She wanted to look for Brian. Her gaze roved over the crowd. Her heart leaped when she spotted him in the center of the room. He was leaning against a pole, wearing his brown leather jacket.

Riley hurried toward him. But then she noticed

that he was talking to a pretty girl. A very pretty girl. *I can't compete with someone like that,* she thought. She started to edge away, hoping Brian hadn't seen her.

Too late.

"Hey, kiddo!" Brian called, waving her over. Riley smiled through clenched teeth. *I hate when he calls me that!* she thought.

"Hey, Brian," she replied, trying not to gaze into his blue eyes for too long. He was *so* cute!

"This is Lydia," Brian told Riley. "Lydia, this is Riley—my mom's best friend's daughter." He elbowed Riley gently. "Right, Riles?"

"That's me. The mom's best friend's daughter." Riley wished she could make herself disappear. Brian still thought of her as a little kid. And Lydia was staring at her as if she were a piece of lint.

Just then Coach Holmes bustled up to them, looking excited. He was followed by a blond woman wearing a blue suit and tortoiseshell glasses. "Team meeting outside, Brian," he announced.

Perfect timing! Riley tried not to look too happy. "Gee, too bad. Just when we were all getting to know each other," she murmured to Lydia. She followed Brian out of the school.

Chloe and the rest of the Model UN team were

already waiting on the front steps. Riley hung back a few paces as Brian joined them.

Coach Holmes led the blond woman forward. "Everyone, this is Julie Watson, from the International Chapter of the Model UN, and she's got some very exciting news," he said.

"Each year we select one school to participate in the International Model UN Competition on a full scholarship," Ms. Watson announced. Riley noticed that she had a British accent. "The competition is in two weeks—in London. And this year we've chosen Lakeview High to participate!"

"*What?*" Chloe yelped.

Ms. Watson smiled at Chloe. "Actually, it's all thanks to you, Chloe," she explained. "Even though your team didn't win first place, I was so impressed with your performance that I decided Lakeview High should attend the competition."

Wow! Riley stared at her twin sister, impressed. *This should cheer Chloe right up!*

Brian stepped in, looking worried. "Ms. Watson, uh, London's kind of expensive, isn't it?"

"Airfare, rooms, meals—everything is covered by the scholarship," Ms. Watson explained.

"Translation—it's free!" Coach Holmes added.

"We're really going to London?" Chloe gasped.

Chloe and Rachel hugged. Dylan did a little dance with his camera. Brian whooped excitedly.

"A chance to rebound from our third place disaster!" Chloe exclaimed.

Riley watched the group celebrate, suddenly feeling like an outsider. *I never thought I'd be jealous of Chloe*, she thought. *Especially not over the Model UN. But now she gets to go to London. With Brian!*

Then she noticed that Randall, the fifth team member, wasn't celebrating. He stepped forward. "Um...guys," he said. "I can't go. My sister's getting married that week. I can't miss her wedding. Sorry."

Ms. Watson frowned. "Oh, dear. That presents a problem," she said. "Each participating team must have five members."

"You mean if Randall doesn't go, the rest of us can't go either?" Chloe asked, her eyes wide.

"I'm afraid not," Ms. Watson agreed. "Unless you can find someone to replace him."

Riley's heart skipped a beat. Maybe she'd just lost her mind, but...

"What about me?" she blurted out.

"*You?*" Chloe stared at Riley.

Riley avoided her gaze. She knew what her sister was thinking, *You're terrible at social studies!*

Coach Holmes beamed. "Terrific idea!" he

declared. "Everyone, let's give a big warm welcome to our newest teammate—Riley Lawrence!"

Brian, Rachel, and Dylan surrounded Riley, welcoming her to the team. But Riley noticed Chloe was hanging back—and she didn't look happy.

As everyone began to talk about the trip, Chloe grabbed Riley's arm and pulled her aside. "I know what you're up to," she whispered.

"What? I love Model UN!" Riley replied, trying to sound innocent. "You get to talk about world issues. Vote on, uh, stuff. You know."

"Come on, admit it," Chloe said. "You're just trying to get closer to Brian."

Riley put her hands on her hips. Chloe's attitude was really starting to annoy her. Okay. So maybe she was right, but that was beside the point. "Did I miss something here, Chloe? Like a 'thanks for volunteering'?"

"This competition means a lot to me," Chloe snapped. "It's not some 'play to play' thing. This is a play to *win* thing." She glared at her sister. "And another thing. If you go all the way to London and *don't* ask Brian out, I'll kill you!" Turning on her heels, she stalked away.

"Thanks, Chloe!" Riley called after her. "Like I'm not under enough pressure already!"

CHAPTER THREE

Chloe stared out the window as the airplane descended into London's Heathrow Airport. London was breathtaking at night—like a perfect golden postcard. *I can't believe I'm here!* she thought.

After going through customs, the team left the airport and piled into their first London taxi—a cool black sedan. Everyone marveled at the sights of the city as they crossed the Thames River.

"Well, team, this is your first moment on foreign soil." Coach Holmes grinned. "Enjoy it, because it's your *last* moment of free time this week. It's time to show the International Model UN that China rules!" Lakeview was representing China at the competition.

The taxi pulled up to the Park Hotel, an elegant brick building near London's famous Hyde Park.

Chloe watched as other Model UN members arrived. Well-dressed kids with laptop computers, electronic pocket organizers, and cell phones filed into the hotel. *They look so confident,* she thought. *So prepared.* She suddenly felt nervous.

She followed her group into the oak-paneled lobby, where kids from all over the world were checking in. Brian, wearing cargo pants and a sweatshirt, eyed the team from Eton, an English boys' school. They all wore stiff white shirts and matching blazers, with their school logo on the pocket. "Whoa!" Brian said.

Riley giggled. "Check it out. Aliens from planet prep school."

Everyone laughed. "Yeah," Brian added. "I thought they only cloned sheep in England."

Chloe smoothed her blouse and adjusted a stray hair. "Come on, guys. This is our chance to make a good impression on the competition."

In the next second, she spotted Dylan, wearing a bright orange Hawaiian shirt, jeans, and a backward baseball cap. He came out of the men's room trailing a long strip of toilet paper from his sneaker. "No," she groaned.

"So much for first impressions," Rachel said.

Chloe watched in horror as Dylan approached a Japanese team. He started chatting to a petite, pretty girl in a short skirt. Chloe could tell from his gestures that he was trying to act cool. And she could tell from the girl's glances at his shoe that it wasn't working—at all.

"Calling 911," Rachel said, pretending to dial a phone.

"Operation Save-the-American," Riley joined in.

"From *himself*," Chloe added, and hurried across the room. She had to get that toilet paper off Dylan's foot!

Chloe dashed up to Dylan as the Japanese girl was walking away. She stepped on the toilet paper, trying to free it from Dylan's shoe.

"I think that girl digs me," Dylan said. "I'm going to check her out. Catch you later."

He trotted off—leaving Chloe with the toilet paper stuck to *her* shoe. She shook her foot. It wouldn't come off. She shook her foot again, harder. No luck.

Finally, Chloe kneeled down to rip the bit of paper off—and found herself staring at a foot in a polished brown loafer.

The foot stepped in and pinned the toilet paper to the floor. Chloe glanced up, then shot to her feet. She was face-to-face with an incredibly gorgeous teenage boy.

"I've got a foot on it," the boy said with a slight smile. He had the most adorable English accent.

"Uh...th-thank you," Chloe stammered. She stood there with her mouth open, then closed it when she realized she must look like an idiot.

"You might want to check your shoes, next time, before you leave the loo," he added with a big grin. He had the cutest dimples!

"Lou who?" Chloe asked, confused.

"The W.C.," he explained. "You know, the loo. The toilet?"

"Oh, *this*." She pointed to the toilet paper. "This isn't mine." She cringed as soon as the words left her mouth. *Nice comeback, Chloe!*

"It was this other guy's," she added, then winced. That didn't help!

The boy raised one eyebrow at her.

"Uh—I think I'll make a quick exit right about now." She backed up. She could barely breathe.

"What's your name?" the boy asked.

"C-C-Chloe," she stuttered.

He smiled, showing those dimples again. "I'm James. James Browning."

"Nice to meet you, James." She waited for him to turn away, but he just stood there looking at her. *He probably thinks I'm totally weird,* she told herself.

"Well, bye." Chloe turned to go—and tripped over a pile of suitcases. She went sprawling on the ground and landed at Riley's feet.

Riley and Rachel rushed over to help her up.

"Please tell me he didn't see that," Chloe whispered through her teeth.

Riley seemed doubtful. "Uh, define 'see.'"

Chloe groaned and buried her head in her hands. *Now he* definitely *thinks I'm weird,* she thought.

Riley patted Chloe on the back. "Come on. Let's check out the rooms."

Chloe's embarrassment faded as she, Rachel, and Riley grabbed their bags and took the elevator up to their floor.

The girls hurried down the hall. "Here it is!" Riley called. She flung open the door to their room.

Make that "hotel cubicle," Chloe thought. The room was a tiny square jammed with furniture. Two double beds, one cot, one night table. No desk. No chair. There was barely enough room to turn around.

Riley counted their bags, then turned back to the room. "Uh, I don't think our bags are going to fit in here," she said. She scratched her head.

"I don't think *we're* going to fit in here," Rachel replied.

"Let's check out the view," Chloe said, trying to make the best of it. She whisked open the drapes— and found herself staring at a brick wall.

Riley gasped. "Oh, no! We have a *real* problem!"

"What's wrong? What?" Chloe cried. Riley

looked absolutely horrified. "Did you see a mouse?"

"Worse!" Riley sank down on the cot. "There's no minifridge," she moaned. "How are we going to have midnight snacks?"

The next morning, the Model UN teams all registered for the competition. Two lines of kids snaked up to a table, where Ms. Watson greeted them.

Riley had spent part of the previous evening scoping out their competitors. She pointed them out as the Lakeview team waited in line.

Riley noticed Dylan nudge Brian. "What a hottie," he whispered, staring at a pretty girl with long, dark hair, standing in the other line.

"That's Gabriela," Riley explained to Chloe and Rachel. "She's with a team from Brazil."

"Yeah." Brian nodded, agreeing with Dylan. He looked over at Gabriela. "I wonder if she has a boyfriend."

Uh-oh, Riley thought. *I hope he doesn't find out!* "Dylan, get a life," she said, pretending not to care that Brian was still looking at the girl.

"I'm working on it." Dylan whipped out his DV cam and went over to Gabriela and her teammates.

Chloe rolled her eyes and turned away. Riley, Brian, and Rachel watched as Dylan struck up a conversation with Gabriela. "So, you're from Brazil. I love those little nuts you guys make," he said.

Gabriela stared at him as if he were an insect.

Riley shook her head. "What a goofball!"

Brian nodded. "Yup. But he's our goofball."

"And you've got to admire the guy," Rachel added with a smile. "He takes risks."

Riley glanced at Brian. Maybe Rachel had a point. If she could only take the risk of telling Brian how she felt, he might realize she wasn't eight years old anymore....

But that would never happen. She just wasn't a risk taker. She sighed and turned her attention back to Dylan.

"So, Gabriela, what country are you guys representing?" Dylan asked.

"China," Gabriela told him.

Chloe whipped around. "Did you say...China?" she demanded.

Gabriela nodded.

Chloe's eyes narrowed. "There must be a mistake. *We're* China."

Gabriela stepped up to Chloe. "The mistake is yours," she said in an icy voice.

Uh-oh! Riley thought. *I think we've got our first international crisis!*

CHAPTER FOUR

The two teams pushed to the head of the line, where Ms. Watson sat at a table with a laptop computer.

"Excuse me," Chloe said. She tried to sound calm. "We've got a problem. Our team and the Brazilian team have both been assigned to represent China."

Ms. Watson's eyes widened, and she began to type away at her computer. "I must apologize," she said after a moment. "There's obviously been a database error." She looked frazzled. "I can't understand how it happened."

"Well, two schools can't represent the same country," Chloe said. "What are we going to do?"

Ms. Watson shook her head.

Coach Holmes stepped forward. "Ms. Watson— this is a Model UN," he said. "Why not let the diplomats work it out?" He nodded toward Chloe and Gabriela.

Chloe raised her eyebrows. She liked the sound

of that! She knew she was a good debater. And she knew she wasn't going to give up China. Not after the two weeks of studying her team already put in!

The teams agreed to negotiate in Gabriela's suite, since the Lakeview team had such tiny rooms. They rode the elevator upstairs, and Gabriela led them to a door marked "Royal Suite."

"Whoa," Riley muttered to Chloe as Gabriela opened the door. "Check this out!"

Wall-to-wall windows drenched the huge room with sunlight. A wide-screen television in an elegant cabinet filled one corner. In another corner was a row of computers. The couches and armchairs looked comfy and inviting. Chloe felt a twinge of envy. Brazil's room was five times bigger than theirs.

"Man...you're rich!" Dylan blurted out.

"Dylan!" Rachel punched him on the shoulder.

Chloe clapped her hands together. "Okay, enough chit-chat. Let's get down to business."

But half an hour later, the two teams had gotten nowhere. Chloe was determined not to give up China—but so was Gabriela. *This is harder than I thought it would be,* Chloe realized. *We could be here for hours!*

Riley had been lounging by the window, looking

more and more bored. Suddenly, she spoke up. "We have a proposal to put on the table," she declared.

Chloe whipped around, startled. "We do?"

Riley nodded. She faced Gabriela. "We'll give you China," she said, her eyes narrowing.

"You will?" Gabriela said, sounding shocked.

"We *will*?" Chloe nearly exploded. What was Riley doing?

"If..." Riley stopped. She smiled as she leaned over and whispered in Gabriela's ear.

Chloe put her head in her hands. She didn't know what Riley's proposal was—but she had a feeling her sister had just ruined everything.

Coach Holmes stood at the entrance to the Royal Suite, amazed. "You got their rooms?"

"Riley traded China for the Royal Suite," Brian said gleefully.

"Plus the key to the fridge," Riley said proudly, dragging a suitcase on wheels past him.

"Not to mention room service," Brian added.

"And DSL connections for the computers. Speed will be crucial," Dylan explained, flopping onto a plush couch.

"Well, at least if we lose, we'll go down in style!" Riley declared.

Chloe stewed in the corner as she watched her teammates move in their bags. She knew everyone was impressed by Riley's so-called negotiation. But Chloe was angry. Sure, the room was bigger and better. But they had given up China. And now they had only two days to learn everything there was to know about a whole other country!

Then Coach Holmes clapped his hands together. "All right, team, I've got good news. I got you guys the United Kingdom—England."

Chloe glanced at her teammates. They looked as unimpressed about this new assignment as she felt.

"Hey, guys," Coach Holmes continued. "It was either that or the Republic of Chad."

The whole team cheered. "Way to go, Coach," Brian said, slapping Dylan a high five.

"Right on, Coach," Dylan said. "But what's the difference between England and the United Kingdom?"

Chloe couldn't keep quiet any longer. "I can't believe this," she said, jumping to her feet. "England is just part of the United Kingdom, along with Northern Ireland, Scotland, and Wales. Anyone who calls all of the UK 'England' is making a mistake."

Then Chloe turned to face Riley. "I don't get it.

Did we come here for room service and the mini-fridge? Or did we come to win this competition?" she demanded.

"Why can't it be a little of both?" Riley asked.

Chloe glared at Riley. "I knew your attitude was going to sink this team."

Riley stepped up to her sister. "*My* attitude? You're the one with the attitude. I mean, we're not actually saving the world, Chloe. This is supposed to be fun!"

"Meow—catfight!" Dylan said, reaching for his camera.

Furious, Chloe whirled and stomped into the bedroom. Nobody except her seemed to get it. Nobody except her seemed to care whether or not they won!

Well, we're going to win anyway, she promised herself. *I'll make sure of that. No matter what!*

CHAPTER FIVE

Riley felt like a trapped animal. She and her teammates had been stuck in the Royal Suite for two days now, studying their new assignment: England.

Two days to cram in two weeks' worth of work, Riley thought. *So much for my brilliant idea to give up China.*

She sat at the computer table between Brian and Dylan, across from Rachel and Chloe. They were all surrounded by books on English history. The garbage pail overflowed with candy wrappers and empty soda cans. Chloe had been pushing them to study nonstop for the last two days. She'd barely even let them get up to go to the bathroom!

Dylan and Rachel were passing a ball back and forth, trading facts and figures. Rachel tossed the ball to Dylan, "Population?" she asked.

"Fifty-nine million," Dylan answered, passing the ball back to her. "Form of government?"

Rachel caught the ball. "Um, let me think.

Constitutional monarchy. Political parties?"

Riley looked over at Brian who was thumbing through newspapers and clipping out articles. Then Riley saw him flip to the sports section. A second later Chloe snatched the paper out of Brian's hands and gave him a stern look. *She sure is tough!* Riley thought.

Riley shifted in her chair again. She couldn't get comfortable. Her left leg had fallen asleep. She stood up and shook it out. Nobody glanced up from their books.

She cleared her throat. Still, nobody looked at her. They were too busy reading. *This is ridiculous!* she thought.

She dropped a book on the floor, loudly.

No one looked up.

Riley couldn't stand it any longer. She jumped up onto the couch and let out a Tarzan yell.

Everyone looked up at her. *Finally.*

In a super-calm voice, Riley declared, "I have to get out of this room. *Now!*"

Brian rose from his seat and slowly approached her. "Easy, girl."

Dylan grabbed his DV cam and zoomed in on Riley's face. "Student goes psycho at UN competition," he said. "Film at eleven."

Chloe shook her head. "This is crunch time, Riles. The other teams have had *weeks* to prepare."

"Chloe, I'm with Riley on this." Rachel spoke up now. "I just can't absorb anymore." She pushed her books aside.

Dylan nodded. "My brain is completely full."

"Somehow I doubt that," Brian said with a laugh.

They're with me! Riley thought. She felt a bubble of excitement. "Guys, all I'm saying is, we're representing England, right? So we're studying England. But we're *in* England."

"*So?*" Chloe asked, sounding impatient.

Riley jumped down from the couch and strode to the window. "So everything we need to know is right out *there*. Waiting for us!" She threw open the curtains, revealing an amazing view of London.

"She's got a point," Dylan said.

"Definitely," Brian agreed.

Riley stared at her sister. *Please, Chloe,* she said silently. *Let us get out of here for a while!*

Chloe suddenly broke into a grin. "Well, you've proved you can debate pretty well when you want to," she admitted.

"Yes!" Riley threw her fist in the air in victory, and everyone grabbed their coats.

● ● ●

Dylan's camera whirred as the team boarded a red double-decker bus and began a whirlwind tour of the city. First stop—the Tower of London.

Chloe read aloud from her guidebook as soon as they got off the bus. "Constructed in 1078, the Tower of London became one of the few centers of royal power. Many of England's most famous prisoners were held within these dank walls."

Riley quickly bought a pretzel from a street vendor as Chloe turned a page.

"That tower over there was built in the thirteenth century." Chloe gazed up at the tall structure. "Wow. That's *so* amazing."

Rachel whistled. "Everything here is so old!"

Riley tried to take a bite of her pretzel, but it was as hard as a rock. "Even this *pretzel* is from the last century," she joked, rubbing her jaw.

Brian laughed. "That was funny, kiddo." He thumped her on the shoulder, then walked on.

Riley rolled her eyes and dumped the pretzel in a trash bin. This "kiddo" thing was really starting to get on her nerves!

"So this was a prison?" Rachel asked.

Chloe nodded. "Yup."

"And a torture chamber," Brian said in a spooky voice.

They filed out onto Tower Green, an outdoor area that was once used for executions. Chloe read from her guidebook. "It says that King Henry the Eighth had two of his wives beheaded on this very spot."

Riley passed the block where the prisoners had to place their heads. An ax rested eerily in its center. "Yuck!" she exclaimed.

Next Chloe led them to the Jewel House, home to the Crown Jewels. As they moved past case after case of crowns encrusted with diamonds and rubies, golden sabers, and necklaces with sparkling gems the size of golf balls, Riley pressed her nose to the glass. *Now, this is interesting!* she thought.

After checking out the rest of the Crown Jewels and the dungeon, the team decided to take a break. They headed back outside and bought lemonade from a snack stand.

Riley and Brian shared a drink. They sat down on a bench outside Tower Green just as a girl in a super-short skirt walked by. Brian's eyes followed her. Annoyed, Riley nudged him.

"It's not very cool to look at other girls when we're talking," she told him.

"We weren't talking. We were drinking," Brian argued. He offered her a sip of lemonade.

"She's not your type," Riley said, taking the cup.

He gave her a doubtful look. "I bet she doesn't like sports," she added.

Brian frowned. "I could *not* hang with a girl who didn't dig sports," he replied. He turned to Riley. "Hey, remember when our dads took us to the Dodger game?"

Riley's heart thumped. Was she finally getting through to him? She decided to help the memory along. "I was ten, you were twelve...."

"And you ate three hot dogs and blew chow all over the guy in front of us!" Brian let out a huge laugh.

Riley wanted to sink right through the bench. "Well, I think we've had enough history for today." She handed Brian the lemonade and stood up.

"Come on, don't be mad. It was funny," Brian called, still laughing.

Riley walked off to catch up with Chloe, who was feeding bread crumbs to some pigeons on the grass.

"What's the matter?" Chloe asked.

"He remembers me as the girl who barfed at the Dodger game." Riley kicked a rock.

"So don't do it again," Chloe said with a smile.

Riley plunked herself onto another bench. She felt so frustrated. So invisible to Brian.

Chloe sat next to her. "Look, Riley, are you here to play? Or are you here to win?" she asked, nodding in Brian's direction.

Riley gazed down at her feet. She crossed then uncrossed them a couple of times. Why was it so hard for her to be bold, when it was so easy for her sister?

"I guess I'm afraid, Chloe," she said at last. "But I know you can't understand that."

Chloe stared at her. "Are you *joking*?" She burst out laughing. "I'm *always* afraid. That's part of life."

Riley couldn't believe what she was hearing. Chloe? Afraid?

"Riley—if you don't try, you won't fail. But you won't succeed, either," Chloe said gently. "Now, quit acting like his little sister and *go* for it."

Riley gazed at Brian. Could she really do it? Could she make the first move? She still wasn't sure.

But there was one thing she *did* know. Sometimes Chloe could be a great sister—and a great friend.

Riley smiled at Chloe. "Thanks," she said softly. "Thanks for listening."

CHAPTER SIX

The cabdriver pulled up in front of Buckingham Palace later that day. "Home to the Queen of England herself!" Dylan said as he filmed the team piling out.

Two guards were positioned at the palace gates, wearing the trademark fuzzy black hats, red jackets, and black pants. The men stood very still, staring off into the distance. Their faces had no expression on them.

"Hey, aren't these the guards who never speak or laugh—no matter what?" Riley asked as they made their way through the gates.

Chloe nodded and read from her book. "It says here that 'rain or shine, heat or cold, the palace guards stand watch without so much as a smile or snicker.'"

Dylan raised his eyebrows. "Sounds like a challenge to me." He pointed his DV cam at his teammates. "And now, making history, these young Americans will attempt to do what has never been done—make one of these guards laugh!"

For the next fifteen minutes, Riley, Chloe, Brian, and Rachel did everything they could think of to make the guards laugh. Brian made goofy faces. Rachel did a silly dance. Riley and Chloe fired off their surefire jokes.

"What do you call a piece of wood with nothing to do?" Riley called. She paused. "Board!" she answered herself, then cracked up.

"How do you make a tissue dance?" Chloe asked. "Put a little boogie in it!"

Chloe was laughing by now, but when she sneaked a peek at the palace guard, his face hadn't moved at all. Not a grin, not a snort, not even a twitch! *Boy, these guys are good!* she thought.

"Oh, well," Riley said, still giggling as they finally gave up. "At least *we* had fun!"

As Chloe, Dylan, Rachel, Brian, and Riley left the palace, Chloe glanced at her sister and her friends. She couldn't remember the last time she'd had so much fun. *We make a pretty great team!*

Next, they headed to Parliament, where England's House of Lords and House of Commons meet. Big Ben, the famous clock, rang out three o'clock just as they arrived.

"This is the legislative branch," Chloe reminded

her teammates. "They pass laws, just like our Congress."

Inside, they took seats in the balcony, watching members of the House of Lords debate down on the floor below. Chloe felt a tingle of excitement. Here she was, in London, witnessing the British government in action!

When the House broke for tea, Chloe gathered her teammates. "Wasn't that amazing?" she asked.

"If you like C-Span," Riley muttered. Brian, Rachel, and Dylan laughed as they started moving toward an exit. Then Rachel let out an excited yelp.

"*There's* something even more interesting," she whispered to Chloe. "Prince Charming at two o'clock!" She pointed ahead of them.

Chloe looked—and nearly choked, as she saw James Browning, the gorgeous boy she'd met in the hotel lobby. He stood near the exit, talking to a silver-haired man in a dark suit.

"Hey, isn't that one of the lords?" Rachel asked.

Chloe nodded. *What is James doing talking to a lord?* she wondered.

As they approached, Chloe overheard part of the conversation.

"How do you expect to win with such half-baked ideas, James?" the man demanded. He shoved some papers at James. "Your proposal needs rethinking."

"My faculty adviser thought it was rather good," James replied.

He sounds kind of upset, Chloe thought.

"Your faculty adviser was never a Member of Parliament, was he?" the man snapped. "James, you have an opportunity to make a mark here. Winning this competition will open doors for you."

"Yes, sir," James said, lowering his head.

An usher whispered something in the lord's ear, and he nodded and hurried off. James glanced up and spotted Chloe. His expression changed from upset to pleased.

"Chloe! What are you doing here?" he asked. "Why aren't you preparing? The competition is tomorrow, you know."

"Actually, this *is* preparation. We're England," Chloe explained. Just looking at James made her feel weak in the knees. *Stay calm, Chloe,* she told herself. "What about you—what are you doing here?"

"Just some family business," James replied.

"Your family's in the *Parliament* business?" she asked, confused.

"My father's a lord," he admitted. "Unfortunately."

That silver-haired man was James's father? Chloe tried not to look too amazed. "Doesn't *sound* unfortunate," she said.

"It's difficult to explain to..." he trailed off.

Chloe folded her arms across her chest. "To what? A *commoner*?"

James winced, obviously embarrassed. "Is this one of those 'quit while I'm ahead' things?" he asked.

Chloe grinned. "No. One of those 'quit while you're *behind*' things," she shot back.

James laughed.

There was a pause. "Well," Chloe said, suddenly feeling awkward again, "I'd better go. We've still got a lot to see today." She motioned to her friends, who were waiting for her at the exit a few yards away.

She started to walk away. "Chloe," James called.

She turned around.

"Would you like a tour guide?" James asked.

"Yes!" Rachel and Riley both shouted before Chloe could even open her mouth to answer.

The six teenagers piled into another big black cab, and James took them to see even more of the sights of London. They stopped at the Globe Theatre, where Shakespeare's plays were first performed. Then they headed for Kensington Gardens, a famous London park.

Riley and Rachel managed to drag Dylan and Brian away so that Chloe could be alone with James. Chloe was grateful to them, but she hoped they weren't being too obvious.

"So," James said, "would you like to see a special spot of mine? It's right nearby." He led Chloe through a clearing to a bronze statue of a boy playing a set of musical pipes. Chloe moved closer to read the sign on the statue's base.

"Peter Pan?" she cried, delighted.

"You're familiar with it?" James asked.

"Are you kidding? I own the video. Saw the play. And read the book. Twice," she confessed. "Peter Pan. The boy who didn't want to grow up."

She studied the statue more closely. Now that she thought about it, the boy looked kind of like James....

Chloe smiled. "Don't you want to grow up, Lord Browning?" she asked playfully, doing her best British accent.

"Do I have a choice, Lady Lawrence?" he asked.

"You could fly off to Neverland," she replied.

"Would you go with me?" he asked, moving closer.

Chloe felt breathless. *I'd go anywhere with you,* she thought.

But somehow she couldn't say it. Instead, she cracked a joke. "As long as I don't have to be Wendy," she replied, flashing a smile. "I don't clean up after lost boys."

"Cut it out." Riley elbowed Brian. "You did that on purpose," she complained.

Riley and Brian were navigating remote-control sailboats on the Round Pond in Hyde Park. Brian kept crashing his boat into hers.

"I can't help it if you're a reckless driver," Brian said. He reached over and tried to grab the controls from her.

"Don't even think about it!" Riley shrieked.

A tug of war broke out. They each had one hand on the control box, laughing as they wrestled with each other.

Riley suddenly found herself looking into Brian's deep blue eyes, and she lost concentration. Without thinking, she let go of the box. Brian flew backward and landed on the grass.

Riley put her hand over her mouth. "Whoops." Then she started to giggle.

Laughing, Brian stood up. He brushed dirt off

his pants. "I'll get you next time, Riles!" he said.

"I hope so," Riley shot back.

Brian looked startled. *Whoa! Did I really just say that?* Riley wondered. She could feel the blood rushing to her cheeks. *What was I thinking?*

A loud quacking sound broke the moment. Riley and Brian turned to see Rachel chasing some ducks across the grass. Dylan followed, busily filming her.

"This extremely weird American bird makes its way across the Atlantic only once in a lifetime for a bizarre mating dance," he narrated.

Riley shook her head, smiling. "Rachel and Dylan are such goofs. They're a perfect couple."

"If only Dylan weren't so clueless," Brian replied.

Riley gave Brian a sidelong glance. He seemed to have totally forgotten what had just happened between them.

She sighed. Unfortunately, it seemed that Dylan wasn't the only clueless one around here!

CHAPTER SEVEN

"This is so exciting!" Chloe said as her team entered the General Assembly room the next morning. It was an auditorium designed to look like the real United Nations. A ring of tables faced a stage with a podium at the center. Each school sat at its own table, with a flag and a nameplate identifying the country it would represent. National flags were hung around the room.

The twenty-five delegations filed in and took their seats. The Lakeview High team took its place at the table labeled "United Kingdom." Chloe spied James sitting across the aisle with the delegation marked "Ireland." She gave him a little wave, and her heart fluttered as he waved back.

Riley sat next to her. "Just remember. He's Ireland. We're England. We've got problems that go back hundreds of years," she teased.

"Don't remind me," Chloe replied. She didn't laugh. Suddenly, she realized she was actually going to be competing against the guy she had a huge crush on. *If he wins, I'll be totally upset,* she thought. *But if I win, he might be mad at me.*

Ms. Watson strode up to the podium. "Ladies and gentlemen. Welcome to day one of the International Model United Nations Competition," she announced. "Over the next four days, you will be evaluated in many activities by our judges." Three judges, seated behind her, waved to the audience.

"Each team will receive points for its performance in speeches, debates, and general behavior," Ms. Watson went on. "You will be judged on how well you represent the views of the country you have been assigned."

Ms. Watson paused, then said, "Life often throws you curveballs." She gave a mysterious smile. "And so will we. As in the real world, you should be prepared for anything."

What does that mean? Chloe wondered.

"As you know, each team was asked to come prepared with a proposal to help end world hunger. Your job this morning is to get your country's proposal passed by winning votes from your fellow nations. This is a test of your ability to convince people of your ideas. Good luck," Ms. Watson said. Then she turned and left the stage.

The competition had begun!

The teams took turns sending a delegate to the podium. Each delegate presented a five-minute proposal on how to end world hunger.

Gabriela spoke for her team. "The People's Republic of China proposes that the problem is not too little food—it's too many people." She went on to explain why their proposal was so important.

Next, James went to the podium. "Ireland believes the use of genetically engineered food can help solve the problem of world hunger...."

Finally, it was Lakeview's turn. Chloe took the podium. "The United Kingdom proposes that we provide farmers around the world with better technology...."

After the presentations, the delegates had one hour to "work" the room—that is, to try to convince as many other delegates as they could that their team's proposal was the best. At the end of the hour, each team would vote, and all the votes would be counted. The only rule was, you couldn't vote for your own team's proposal.

Chloe gathered her teammates together for a pep talk. "Okay, guys. This is it...." She stopped when she noticed her sister glancing nervously around the room. "Riley, pay attention. This is important."

"I know, but...it's just that everyone looks so together," she said. "Maybe I *shouldn't* have traded China for the suite. I mean, I can't remember anything I studied."

Chloe put a hand on her sister's shoulder. "Look. I know the other teams are more prepared than we are. But we've got something they don't."

"What?" Rachel asked.

Chloe pulled a bag from her backpack and grinned. "Potato chips."

"You mean crisps?" Dylan said. "Isn't that what they call them in England?"

"You got it!" Chloe cried. "Here's what we're going to do." She turned to Rachel. "Rachel, I hear the Finnish delegation is sponsored by a health food nut. I bet that team is dying for some junk food," she said, handing Rachel the bag of potato chips. "See what you can do with these. Dylan, you've got your Game Boy with you, don't you?"

"Check, chief." Dylan held up a video game player. "I'll find a way to use it."

"Okay." Chloe handed Riley some fashion magazines. "Riley, you're tackling Gabriela's team. You know what to do, people. Let's move!" she ordered.

In moments, the room was buzzing as the young diplomats began wheeling and dealing.

Chloe found herself talking to a goofy-looking delegate with spiked hair. While she gave him her sales pitch, she scanned the room. She saw Rachel munching chips with the Finnish delegation, while Riley and Gabriela sat with their heads together over a fashion magazine. So far, so good! She turned her attention back to the boy in front of her.

"Can we count on your vote, then?" she asked.

"If you dance with me at tonight's party," he said.

Chloe thought fast. "Sorry, I'm booked. But my sister would love to," she offered with a smile.

One hour later, Ms. Watson approached the podium again. The delegates took their seats.

"Delegates, the votes have been tallied. The country with the most votes for its proposal is...the United Kingdom!"

Yes! Chloe and her teammates hugged and high-fived.

Angry mutters ran through the room. Then one of James's teammates raised his hand.

"England cheated," he complained. "They're supposed to negotiate, but instead they traded junk food and fashion magazines for votes."

"Uh-oh," Riley whispered. "Looks like we made enemies."

Chloe shook her head. "This is part of the game. We didn't do anything wrong," she said firmly.

"Yeah, well, tell that to all of them," Dylan said. He panned his DV cam around the room at the other delegates.

"If looks could kill..." Rachel winced.

"We'd be goners," Brian finished.

Ms. Watson scanned the rule book, her brow furrowed. "They didn't exactly break the rules. They...seem to have just *bent* them."

The angry mutters broke out again. Ms. Watson raised both hands. "You may not like their methods, but they achieved their goal," she said.

"See," said Chloe. "We won, fair and square."

Still grumbling, the delegates began to trickle out of the room. Chloe caught James's eye and gave him a triumphant grin.

He didn't smile back.

Chloe swallowed hard. *I won,* she thought. *So why do I feel as though I've lost?*

CHAPTER EIGHT

That night, all the delegates met up at a teen dance club in London's Soho district. Riley had tried on three outfits before she decided on her favorite black skirt and a sparkly pink tank top. She was going to make Brian notice her tonight if it killed her!

As the Lakeview team entered the club, Riley couldn't help noticing the cold stares from some of the other delegates. *I guess they're still mad about the way we won this afternoon,* she thought, glancing at her sister. *I probably would be, too. It was kind of sneaky, I guess.*

Riley's thoughts were interrupted when Chloe grabbed her arm. Hard. "Ouch! Watch it, Chloe," Riley said.

"James is headed this way," her sister whispered. "I hope he's not mad at me."

Riley did, too. She knew how much her sister liked him. Chloe practically glowed when he reached them.

James said hello to both of them, but he didn't take his eyes off Chloe. "Want to dance?" he asked her. Chloe nodded. Then she followed James onto the packed dance floor.

"Uh, bye," Riley said to their backs. *Well, I guess if he was mad about this afternoon, he's over it now,* she thought.

Riley was happy for her sister, but as she moved to the edge of the dance floor, she felt totally alone. Everyone else seemed to be having fun. Even Dylan and Rachel were out there!

Then Brian walked by, talking to Gabriela. Riley took a deep breath. Enough feeling sorry for herself. It was time to go out and get the guy she wanted!

Before she could change her mind, Riley ran after Brian and took his arm.

"Brian," she heard herself say, "would you like to dance?"

"Uh, no," he replied.

"Oh." Riley froze, horrified. *He turned me down!*

"I mean..." Brian looked embarrassed. "Uh, unless I have a football and five guys chasing me, I don't, you know, move so well."

Oh. Riley felt a huge wave of relief. "So, pretend you're being chased," she suggested.

He frowned. "By who?"

"By me." Whoops—she did it again! *Did those words really come out of my mouth?* Riley wondered. She was glad the club was dark, so no one could see how red her cheeks were turning.

Oh, well. Too late to take it back now, she decided. She took Brian's hand and led him onto the dance floor. *Breathe deeply, Riles,* she told herself.

Brian twisted on the dance floor, giving it his all. But Riley barely noticed his dancing, she was so focused on his adorable face just inches from hers.

Then the music changed to a slow song. "Thanks, kiddo," Brian said, and began to walk off the floor.

Do it! Riley told herself. *Make your move!* "Brian!" she called after him.

He turned around.

"Don't you want to learn to slow-dance?" She smiled.

Brian blinked, then smiled. "Uh—sure." He stepped toward Riley, put his arm around her waist, and took her right hand in his. He rested his cheek on top of her head as they began to dance.

Riley's heart almost leaped out of her chest. She was in heaven!

"Uh…excuse me." A boy with spiked hair tapped Riley on the shoulder. "I gave your team my vote this afternoon because your sister said you would dance with me," he said. He pointed to Chloe, who was dancing nearby.

Brian frowned and stepped back. "No problem," he said, shrugging. "I'll catch you later, Riles."

No! Riley wanted to shout. She shot her sister a dirty look. Chloe waved guiltily.

"A deal's a deal," Riley said gloomily. She put her hands on Spike Boy's shoulders and started to sway.

Chloe and James watched as Brian walked away. Chloe saw Riley staring after him.

"Your sister's got it bad for Brian," James said.

"Is it that obvious?" Chloe asked.

"The drooling is kind of a giveaway," he joked.

Chloe giggled.

"So, what about you two?" he asked. He gestured toward Riley. "Do you get along?"

"Yeah—as long as we're not in the same room," Chloe cracked. "We're very different. She just wants to have fun and hang out with boys." As soon as the words were out of her mouth, she realized how they sounded. "Uh—not that there's anything wrong with that!" she added quickly.

James smiled and tightened his arms around her waist. Chloe gulped. She'd never had a crush on someone she was competing against before. This could get complicated!

"James, you should know something about me. I play to win," she said.

He gave her a funny look. "As do I," he replied. "Although we choose to play differently."

"I don't want this competition to get in the way of our—" She stopped.

"Our what?" he asked softly.

"Of...us," she said. There. It was out!

"It can get in the way only if we let it," he replied.

"Right," Chloe said. She laid her head down on James's shoulder.

She hoped it was that simple!

CHAPTER NINE

The next day, the delegates were all invited to a garden party and polo match at James's house. Chloe was looking forward to seeing where he lived. But when the buses finally pulled onto a circular driveway, she wasn't prepared for what she saw.

His house is an estate! she realized. She gazed at the huge stone mansion surrounded by rolling green lawns and formal gardens.

"Whoa. This dude has some serious bucks!" Dylan exclaimed. He belched loudly. "'Scuse me."

"*Dylan!*" Riley, Chloe, and Rachel all said together.

"What?" he demanded. "I *said* excuse me."

James's father, Lord Browning, stood on the lawn shaking hands with the delegates. Chloe was about to get in line, when James took her arm. He was dressed in riding pants and a charcoal-gray shirt. Chloe thought she'd never seen anyone so gorgeous.

"Let me give you a tour," he suggested.

She was happy to go. But she couldn't help

noticing that Lord Browning shot her an angry glare. "I don't think your father approves of me," she said.

She meant it as a joke, but James seemed uncomfortable. "Father doesn't approve of much," he mumbled. "Don't let it bother you."

Hmmm. What's that about? Chloe wondered. *Does his father think I'm not good enough or something?*

James bit his lip and changed the subject. "So, you've never been to a polo match?"

"Polo—not real big in my hometown. My dad wears the shirts sometimes," Chloe joked.

James laughed. "Mine, too."

They walked around for a few minutes. Then James checked his watch. "We'd better get back," he said. "The match will be starting any minute, and I'm playing in it."

The polo ground was set up on the sweeping lawn behind the mansion. A buffet table on the sidelines was covered with a starched white tablecloth and set with silver and china. Riley, Brian, Rachel, Dylan, and Coach Holmes were already parked next to it, helping themselves to tea cakes, scones, and sandwiches.

Chloe squeezed in next to Dylan, who was piling

dainty tea sandwiches sky high on his plate. "With a place like this, you'd think they could afford regular-size sandwiches," he grumbled.

Chloe shook her head. Dylan was so clueless!

Just then Lord Browning rang a small silver bell. "Good afternoon, ladies and gentlemen," he called. "Welcome to Browning Manor. It is our pleasure to host this reception for the International Model United Nations Competition. Now, if you'll turn your attention to the polo field, we can begin the entertainment."

Chloe watched as eight players on horses thundered across the lush green lawn. She picked out James immediately. He galloped down the field at top speed, then swung his mallet, trying to knock a little white ball through the goalposts at the far end of the field.

Brian scratched his head. "I don't get it. This is a sport? Riding on a horse, chasing a little ball?"

"I know it looks simple," Mr. Holmes explained, "but polo takes years of practice."

Chloe nodded. She could tell by the way he rode that James had been playing all his life.

Wham! James smacked the ball down the field, then chased after it. But just as he was about to swing, a player from the other team galloped in and cut him off. James reined in his horse to avoid a collision. The other player sent the ball flying down the field to a teammate, who whacked it through the goalposts.

"Oh!" Chloe stamped her foot in frustration.

During a break, James rode over to Chloe. He pulled off his riding helmet. "What did you think?" he asked.

"Nice moves, but why did you back off when that guy rode in front of you? You had the ball," Chloe asked.

"You can ride a player off, but you can't charge him. It's against the rules. And polo is a game of *rules*, not loopholes," he added, giving her a sideways look.

"Do I hear the cry of yesterday's sore loser?" she shot back.

"Unlike most of your American games, polo is an artful sport," James said in a superior voice.

Chloe's eyes narrowed. Those were fighting words. Maybe he was angry about yesterday after all. "It doesn't seem too hard," she said carelessly. "Sort of like croquet, but on horses."

James's eyebrows went up. "Maybe you'd like to give it a try?" he asked.

"Sure!" Chloe said. She never turned down a challenge.

Riley stared at her. "Are you crazy?"

Chloe gulped as she realized what she'd gotten into. *Maybe I am!* she thought.

"How did I get dragged into this, anyway?" Riley moaned.

Chloe glanced at her sister as they mounted two of Lord Browning's polo ponies. "You're my sister—that's how!" she said with a grin. But inside, her stomach was churning. She knew she was a good rider, but was she good enough to play polo?

Chloe stared at the faces on the sidelines as she and Riley trotted onto the field—Coach Holmes, Brian, Dylan, Rachel, Lord Browning. Not to mention all the other delegates. She knew she had to be impressive. She had to show them her game was as good as her talk!

"Ready?" she asked Riley.

"No." Riley sighed. "But that never stopped you before."

Then the whistle blew and the game was on.

Chloe rode straight toward James. She swung her horse around his and knocked the ball to Riley out on the wing. Riley hooked mallets with an opposing player and miraculously gained control of the ball.

"Ahh!" Riley screamed. Chloe grinned as her sister galloped madly down the field. Then a player from the other team galloped toward Riley.

"Yikes!" Riley yelled, and passed the ball to Chloe.

Chloe wound up, took a wild swing...and missed the ball completely. Her mallet flew out of her hand and hurtled through the air!

"Heads up!" she shouted as the mallet splashed into the crystal punch bowl on the sidelines. Bright red punch sprayed up, drenching a very proper-looking woman who stood nearby. Chloe was mortified!

Her cheeks flamed as she rode over to the buffet table to retrieve her mallet. *Maybe I should just give up and fade away quietly,* she thought. *Before I do some real damage.*

Then James rode over to her, grinning. "So, are we finished yet?" he asked.

His smug smile made Chloe's blood boil all over again. "Finished?" she snapped. "That was just a warm-up."

With that, the whistle blew and the game was under way again. James got control of the ball and raced toward his goal. But Chloe caught up with him and swiped the ball away. James wasn't smiling anymore. He charged down the field after her, but it was too late. She galloped down the field at top speed and knocked the ball between the posts. "Score!" she yelled.

The crowd on the sidelines cheered. *I did it!* Chloe thought triumphantly. *I showed them all!* Caught up in the moment, she yanked the reins so that her horse reared up on his hind legs. She swung the mallet over her head and let go—on purpose this time. The mallet flew out of her hand and sailed over the heads of the crowd.

The cheers died away. There was a moment of silence. Suddenly Chloe noticed that many of the spectators were shaking their heads and frowning at her. Especially Lord Browning.

Whoops. She'd forgotten that the English were nuts about good sportsmanship.

Then she scanned the field for James. But when she caught his eye, even he shook his head and turned away.

Oh, no. Chloe suddenly felt a stab of worry. James was obviously upset with her, too. But what was the big deal? She had made a great shot. Didn't she deserve to be happy about it?

But maybe this was the wrong place to show off.

• • •

That night, neither Chloe nor Riley was in the mood to hang out with the other delegates at the hotel. Instead, they took a walk through downtown London.

"I can't believe James is so mad at me," Chloe said. "He barely even said good-bye when we left his house."

Riley gazed at her sister in disbelief. Chloe just didn't get it! She had to figure out a way to clue her in.

They stopped to check out a street vendor's jewelry. Chloe picked up a pretty silver ring set with a small blue sapphire. Riley picked up a similar one, but set with a red garnet. She turned it around while she thought about what to say.

"Chloe," she said at last, "people who have to win at all costs turn out to be losers in the end. Because no one wants to be around them." She glanced at her sister.

Chloe looked stung. "I'd rather do something well than do *nothing*," she said stiffly. "As in having a crush on Brian, chasing him to London, then doing absolutely nothing about it!"

Riley felt a surge of anger. Why did Chloe always think her way was the *right* way? So what if she didn't rush into things head-on like Chloe did. So what if she wanted to take things slowly with Brian. Riley glared at her sister. "I guess *nothing* is the only thing I do better than you," she said.

Chloe scowled and turned to the jewelry seller. "I'll take the blue ring," she said, pulling out her wallet.

Riley took out her wallet, too. "I'll take the red."

The woman smiled as she wrapped up the rings. "By the way, girls, they're friendship rings," she said.

The girls exchanged a startled look. After a second, Riley cracked a sorrowful grin. She hated fighting with her sister, but sometimes she just couldn't help it.

"Let's hope they work," she said.

And the girls laughed together.

CHAPTER TEN

The next morning, Ms. Watson took her place at the podium in the General Assembly room. "Welcome to day three of the competition, everyone," she said. "Today's exercise will revolve around dealing with crisis situations."

Chloe barely heard her. She was busy trying to make eye contact with James, who sat across the room. She could tell he was avoiding her gaze.

Chloe felt awful about what happened at the polo match. Her talk with Riley had made her realize just how her behavior must have looked to James. She *had* to get him alone—to apologize.

At that moment, the door to the auditorium burst open. Two men in ski masks and camouflage fatigues stormed down the aisle.

The room fell silent. Chloe was stunned. *What is this?* She whirled and looked at the men again. They carried huge, scary-looking, hot-pink machine guns.

Wait. *Hot pink?*

"They're Super Soakers!" someone yelled.

The masked men aimed, and streams of water shot out of the hot-pink guns. The room erupted into laughter. Kids screamed and laughed as they dodged the water guns. *It's part of the exercise!* Chloe realized. *They're pretending to be terrorists!* She had to smile. Ms. Watson had warned that there would be curveballs. This definitely qualified as one.

The masked men moved down the aisle. They tapped a guy named Niko, then Gabriela, then James, and led them out of the room. As one of the masked men reached England, he tapped Riley.

Wait! Here's my chance to talk to James! Chloe realized. She threw herself in front of her sister. "Take me!" she cried.

"Talk about a drama queen!" Riley grumbled behind her.

The masked men led Chloe, James, Niko, and Gabriela to a room on the eleventh floor of the hotel. Then the shorter of the two men said in a familiar voice, " 'Bye. Have fun." He pulled off his mask. It was Coach Holmes!

"Coach, what are we supposed to do in here? Read magazines and play video games?" Chloe asked.

"Sounds good to me!" Niko grinned.

Ms. Watson bustled in. "It all depends how the hostage negotiations go," she said. She handed a stack of scripts to James. "Everything you need to know is in these scripts," she promised. "If you have any questions, Mr. Holmes will be right outside, guarding the door." She whisked out again before anyone could say anything.

Chloe sneaked a glance at James. They were going to be stuck in this room for a while, Chloe guessed. It was her best chance to talk to him.

"We'd better read these," James said. He handed Chloe a script.

"Thanks," she said. He nodded, then took a chair by the window. *As far from me as possible,* she thought with a pang.

Their first instruction was to call the General Assembly. James picked up the phone and read from the script as the delegates all listened on a speakerphone.

"We're being held hostage. And until the United Nations can convince its members to destroy all nuclear weapons, we will be held in captivity, under terrible conditions," he said.

Chloe glanced around the room. Gabriela was nibbling on some grapes from the minifridge. Niko was playing a video game. She grinned.

I'm Riley Lawrence—and this is my sister, Chloe.

We were picked to go to London—for the International
Model United Nations! All our friends were going, too.

London was amazing! We had a blast hanging with the other kids. And we checked out all the major sights.

We went to the Tower of London, Westminster Abbey, and...

Buckingham Palace. That's where Brian, my major crush, took this picture of me. (No wonder I look so happy!)

We also went to the coolest teen dance club!

The sightseeing was a lot of fun. But you know what the best part was? Yup...the boys! Chloe met a totally cool English guy named James.

He invited us to his huge mansion for the afternoon.

While we were there, Chloe talked me into playing polo. Yikes!

In the end, everything worked out great. We won the Model UN competition! And we even managed to land the boys of our dreams. (Aren't they cute?)

The whole trip was great—but traveling with my sister was the best!

Pretty terrible conditions—not!

James hung up the phone. Gabriela immediately picked up the receiver. "Let's order room service. Being a hostage makes me hungry," she said.

While she ordered, Chloe moved closer to James. "Can we talk? About yesterday?" she asked quietly.

James shrugged. "What's there to talk about?"

"What I did was totally out of line—" Chloe began.

James cut her off. "It's not *what* you did, Chloe. It's the way you did it. Whatever happened to the American notion of 'how you play the game'?"

"I—I don't know..." she stammered. Then she stopped, frowning. Maybe she did know.

"Hopscotch happened," she said slowly. "And spelling bees. And soccer." Chloe bit her lip. "I was always so good, James. People expected I'd win. And when I didn't, all I could see was their disappointed faces."

James didn't say anything.

Chloe swallowed hard and went on. "I hated that, so I made sure I won. And I guess, finally...the rush of winning became the most important thing."

"And you forgot why you even liked playing in the first place," James added softly.

Chloe nodded. Her throat felt tight. Now she saw that she had lost sight of what was really important.

"Other people's expectations can be hard," James said. Chloe was pretty sure he was thinking about his own father.

"But you're about more than winning, Chloe," James said. He took her hand. "We both are."

Back in the General Assembly room, the delegates were trying to figure out how to get the mock terrorists to release their hostages.

Jonathan, from the Eton team, stood up and addressed the room. "Ireland cannot negotiate with terrorists!"

A girl from the Iraqi delegation also stood up. "Their demands are unreasonable!"

Why doesn't Chloe say something smart? Riley wondered. Then she remembered—oh, right, Chloe had been taken hostage. She gulped. *I guess it's up to me!*

Nervously, Riley stood up. "Ridding the world of nuclear weapons...what's so unreasonable about that?" she began. Her mouth went dry as everyone turned to stare at her. But she went on. "I mean, who really needs nuclear weapons, anyway?"

There was a pause. Then the delegates from Iraq and Pakistan raised their hands. A moment later, hands began to pop up around the room. Then everyone began to talk at once.

Riley sank back into her seat, defeated. Brian leaned over and patted her on the back. "Nice try, Riles."

"Now what?" she wondered aloud.

Brian shrugged. "We could send in a SWAT team."

"I could practice my tae kwon do," Dylan added. He leaped into a martial arts pose. "Ha-*ya*!"

Rachel rolled her eyes. "Guys, we're supposed to be peacemakers. Not war makers."

That's when it hit Riley. "Wait. We're supposed to do what our country would do if this were really happening, right?" she asked.

Her teammates nodded.

"So, what would the British do in this situation?" Riley flashed a grin. "Send in their best!"

Dylan's eyes lit up. "Bond," he said in his best English accent.

"James Bond!" Brian, Rachel, and Riley all cried out at once.

"Let's go," Riley whispered to Brian. She had an idea.

A moment later, Riley and Brian slipped out of

the General Assembly room and raced down the hallway. "Where to?" Brian asked, breathless.

"Ms. Watson's room," Riley answered. "It's the logical place."

They rode the elevator to the eleventh floor. Sure enough, Coach Holmes was parked outside Ms. Watson's room, reading the newspaper. "Jackpot," Riley whispered as the two peered around the corner.

Coach Holmes glanced up from his paper. *He heard us!* Riley thought. She gasped and pushed Brian into a nearby supply closet. Then she dove in after him.

"Let's take Coach Holmes down." Brian grabbed spray bottles of cleanser in both hands.

"With cleaning products?" Riley asked.

Brian stared at the air duct on the ceiling. Then he looked at Riley with a gleam in his eye.

"Oh, no. I'm not going up there," she protested.

"Come on, we're James Bond. This is what we do!" He grabbed a stepladder that was leaning against the wall, climbed up, and began to unscrew the grating. Before she knew it, Brian's hand was dangling from the air duct, reaching for hers.

On their hands and knees, they crawled through the dusty vent system. "This is so cool!" Brian exclaimed.

Riley had to smile. *Cool* wasn't exactly the word she would have used. But at least they were alone.

If I were Chloe, I'd grab my chance and kiss him, she thought. She sighed. *But I'm not Chloe.*

"There they are! We found the hostages!" Brian whispered. He stared down through a grate, then turned and grinned triumphantly at Riley. "High-five, kiddo!"

Riley froze. There was that word again. *Kiddo.* She couldn't stand it, not for one more second.

"Brian," she said firmly.

"Yeah?" He stopped fiddling with the grate and turned around. He looked straight into Riley's eyes. Their faces were only inches apart.

Riley felt her heart thumping in her chest as she held his gaze. "Brian," she said softly, "the name's Riley."

Brian just stared at her. "Riley," he repeated slowly.

Riley nodded. She could feel her heart beating harder. *What is he thinking?* she wondered. *He's acting so weird. As if it's the first time he's ever seen me or something.*

And then it happened.

Brian leaned in and gently kissed her.

Riley closed her eyes. His lips were warm and

sweet. She wished this moment would last forever.

Brian pulled away and looked at her. "We'll pick this up later," he whispered, pushing a stray hair off Riley's face. He flashed her a smile. "After all, Bond doesn't get the girl till the end of the movie."

Riley felt as if she were floating. *He kissed me!* she told herself over and over again. *He finally kissed me!*

A moment later they climbed out of the vent duct into Ms. Watson's bathroom.

Riley peeked around the bathroom door. Chloe was talking to Coach Holmes. Luckily, his back was to the bathroom. Riley waved frantically, trying to catch her sister's attention. Finally, Chloe saw Riley over the coach's shoulder.

"Uh, Coach, I'll be back in a moment," Chloe announced loudly. She slipped behind the bathroom door. Riley gestured to the others. One by one, they escaped.

Soon they were all in the air duct and on their way back to the conference. They were free!

A few minutes later, Riley and Brian led the "hostages" into the General Assembly room. Riley strode down the aisle. "Madam Secretary General," she called to Ms. Watson, "England has rescued your diplomats and returned them—safe and sound!"

The room erupted into confusion.

"My goodness! I've been doing this for ten years. We've never had a team actually stage a rescue of any sort," Ms. Watson declared.

"It's not fair," a boy from another team grumbled. "We were supposed to work this out through negotiation."

Ms. Watson shook her head. "You were supposed to work it out. I never said *how*." She smiled at Riley and Brian. "Actually, I thought this was creative problem solving."

Riley stood tall. "Talk is fine. But when negotiations fail, sometimes you have to take action. And Britain does not negotiate with terrorists!" she declared.

The other delegates burst into cheers. Riley glanced at the judges. They looked impressed.

Coach Holmes had slipped in while Riley was making her speech. "Well done, England," he said proudly. Then he wrinkled his brow. "How did you get past me, anyway?"

Riley grinned. "We'll never tell!"

CHAPTER ELEVEN

That night, all the delegates were invited to a boat party on the Thames. Riley, Chloe, and Rachel were getting ready in their room. Riley had on a black cocktail dress. Chloe picked out a red minidress with matching boots. Rachel wore a green vintage sweater with sequins and a black skirt.

"Wasn't that awesome today?" Riley beamed as she put on eye shadow. "I love Model UN!"

Rachel and Chloe exchanged a glance. *Is that my sister talking?* Chloe wondered. Then her eyes narrowed in suspicion.

"Uh, Riles," she said, folding her arms, "what *exactly* happened while you were up there in the air vent with Brian?"

Riley shrugged. "Hey, I don't kiss and tell."

"You *kissed*?" Chloe and Rachel both yelled.

A huge grin broke over Riley's face. "Yes!" she squealed.

Chloe threw down her hairbrush and hugged Riley.

"Finally!" Rachel exclaimed.

"I can't believe it," Chloe said.

Riley looked at her sister. "What about James? Is everything okay with you two?" she asked.

"I think so. We didn't get a chance to finish talking," Chloe said. She hesitated.

Rachel finished putting on her lip gloss. "So finish tonight, at the party."

"He's not coming," Chloe admitted.

"*What?*" Rachel and Riley shrieked.

Chloe sighed and flopped down on the couch. She was feeling a little sorry for herself. "He's having dinner with his father at an all-men's club. I get the feeling his father doesn't think I'm good enough for him," she said. She curled up and pulled a blanket over herself. "Maybe I'll just stay in tonight."

"But...tomorrow's our last day in London," Rachel said.

"Tell me about it," Chloe said, feeling even sorrier for herself. She propped a pillow under her head.

"Hey!" Riley pulled the blanket off Chloe. "What happened to Chloe Lawrence, the girl who plays to win?"

Chloe pulled the blanket back up and sighed. "She got knocked off her high horse. At a polo match."

Riley whipped the covers away again. "This is no time for sulking," she said. "Get back on that horse, girl. I've got a plan!"

"This is the place," Chloe said. She glanced at Riley. "Are you sure this will work?"

"Positive," Riley said. She marched up the steps of Grey's, Lord Browning's club, and pushed open the heavy wooden door.

Grey's was one of London's oldest, stuffiest all-men's clubs. As Riley looked around, she saw dozens of men lounging in leather chairs, reading newspapers, and drinking brandy from big balloon glasses.

The maître d', an elderly man in a dark suit and tie, hurried over to Chloe and Riley. He stared down his nose at them.

"May I help you...er...gentlemen?" he asked.

Gentlemen? Riley glanced down at herself. Oh, right. For a second, she'd forgotten that she and Chloe were dressed up as boys! They'd borrowed jackets and ties from Brian and had tucked their hair up into two of Dylan's baseball caps.

Riley made her voice as deep as she could. "We're guests of Master Browning's," she said in her best English accent.

The maître d' raised an eyebrow. "I see. This way," he said, and led them toward the back of the club.

"See how easy this is?" Riley whispered to Chloe as they followed. Then Riley tripped. A few strands of long, blond hair slipped out from under her cap. "Whoops!" She quickly stuffed it back in place.

The maître d' dropped them off in a back room. Then he left.

"There they are," Chloe said. She pointed to a corner table, where James sat with Lord Browning.

"The judges put a lot of weight on a strong finish. I assume *you'll* be taking the oral essay question for your team," Lord Browning was saying as they walked up. "Give them a reason to be impressed."

"I'll do my best," James replied.

Lord Browning frowned. "Let's hope that's good enough."

Wow, he sure is tough on poor James! Riley thought. *I bet James will be glad to get away.*

She cleared her throat loudly. James looked up. As he caught sight of the girls in their borrowed clothes, his eyes went wide. Riley tried to beam him a mental message. *Don't blow our cover!*

James must have gotten it. "Father, your glasses

73

are filthy. Let me clean them for you," he said, and snatched the glasses right off Lord Browning's nose.

Nice move! Riley thought.

"Oh, what a surprise!" James added. "Father, here are a couple of schoolmates of mine—uh, from Eton," he said.

Lord Browning squinted, but he was obviously very nearsighted without his glasses.

"My name's Colin," Chloe said in a gruff voice.

Riley coughed. "And I'm, uh, Chester."

"Won't you join us for dessert?" Lord Browning said, taking his glasses back from James.

"No!" Riley, Chloe, and James all cried together.

"We're, uh, supposed to review some stuff for tomorrow," Chloe added.

"That's right," James said quickly. "I'd almost forgotten." He jumped up from his seat. "Well, I won't be home too late, Father. Let's go, lads!"

Riley and Chloe mumbled their good nights. Then the three of them hurried out. Riley was concentrating so hard on not laughing that she barely noticed that Chloe's hair was falling out of her cap.

Behind them, Lord Browning put his glasses back on. He stared after them. His eyes narrowed.

"Her," he growled as he recognized Chloe. That American girl was taking up entirely too much of James's time.

He would have to do something about her!

The big boat cruised down the Thames. Chloe and James leaned over the railing, looking across the water at Parliament, which was all lit up.

They were alone.

"Thanks for rescuing me tonight. I don't get to do this very often. Have fun, I mean," James said. He sighed. "Father's always pushing me to do something or other."

Chloe smiled. "Our parents got to be young. Now it's our turn."

"I agree," he said, and put his arm around her.

Chloe's skin tingled. "Although growing up definitely has its advantages," she said softly, looking up at him.

"Definitely," James said, nodding.

Then he leaned down—and kissed her. Chloe closed her eyes. There could never be a more perfect moment!

When the kiss ended, Chloe leaned against James's chest. They looked out across the moonlit city.

"Right there." Chloe pointed across the water. "That's where they flew."

"Who?" James asked.

"Peter Pan and Wendy," Chloe told him.

James smiled. "Second star to the right and then straight on till morning."

"Exactly," Chloe agreed.

At the other end of the deck, Riley and Brian had found a spot where they could be alone, too.

"Years?" Brian said in disbelief.

"Years," Riley confirmed.

"You've had a crush on me for *years*? Am I the lamest, or what?" Brian shook his head. "Well. We should make up for lost time, then!"

He leaned in to kiss her. Then Riley caught a glimpse of light from behind Brian. *What is that?* she wondered, pulling away.

Then she knew what it was. She sighed. "Hold on a minute."

Riley marched over to the shadows, where Dylan was lurking with his DV cam. She leaned in and fogged up his camera with her breath. "Get a life, Dylan!" she cried.

"Riles!" Dylan yelped.

Rachel came up beside him. "She's right, Dylan.

I mean, the whole world's coupled up," she said. "And we're..." She trailed off gloomily.

Then Dylan did something totally surprising. He put his camera down and planted a big kiss on Rachel's lips!

"Whoa!" Rachel gasped. But she was smiling.

Riley grinned and moved back to Brian. "What took you two so long?" she called out to them.

Brian laughed. "Now, where were we?" he asked, taking her in his arms.

She turned her face up to his. "Right about here," she said softly.

Brian kissed her. And Riley felt all was well with the world. Make that...the universe!

CHAPTER TWELVE

Chloe stared into the mirror. The oral essay part of the competition was today, and she should be reviewing her speech. But somehow, she couldn't think about anything except James! The way he looked, the way he kissed...

Uh-oh. "Focus, Chloe," she said to herself.

The doorbell rang. A moment later, Rachel handed Chloe an envelope. "The bellboy brought this for you," she said.

"It's from James," Chloe said, surprised. She scanned the note. "Oh, no! He had a fight with his father." Poor James! She looked up at Riley and Rachel. "He wants me to meet him at Buckingham Palace."

"Now?" Rachel asked.

"We have to be downstairs in ten minutes for the final round," Riley pointed out.

"You guys can manage without me. You'll do great." Chloe grabbed her coat and headed for the door.

"Hello?" Riley said loudly. "There's a trophy calling your name downstairs, Chloe."

Chloe shrugged. A grin spread over her face. "And for the first time, Riles, I just don't hear it."

Then she turned and hurried out the door. James was waiting!

Twenty minutes later, Chloe was the one who was waiting. She stood next to the guard's station in front of Buckingham Palace. Rain pelted against her umbrella and dripped onto her shoes.

Where is James? she wondered for the hundredth time. She couldn't believe he would stand her up. That wasn't like him.

Was it?

"You don't think anything happened to him?" Chloe asked the motionless guard.

The guard stared straight ahead and didn't answer.

Where could he be? she asked herself. *Where?*

Finally, she gave up and wandered away in the pouring rain.

Riley paced up and down in the General Assembly room. Her stomach was churning. Somehow the team was going to have to make it through the final round of the competition without Chloe. Could they do it?

She glanced over at Brian, then Dylan, then Rachel. They looked so serious. They might not seem as dedicated as Chloe. But she knew they really did want to win.

So do I, Riley realized. *I want to win this!*

Then she did a double take. James was walking into the room!

She ran to him. "What are *you* doing here?" she demanded.

"What do you mean?" James asked.

"Uh, James—didn't you write a note to Chloe asking her to meet you at Buckingham Palace this morning?" Riley asked, slightly panicked.

James stared at her. "I didn't write any note. What are you talking about?"

"But I saw your stationery," Riley objected.

Out of the corner of her eye, Riley spotted Lord Browning. He was motioning James to take his seat. Riley glanced at him—and suddenly an idea popped into her mind. A totally horrible idea.

"James, I think maybe you should ask *him* for some answers," she said, nodding toward Lord Browning.

James turned and stared at his father. Lord Browning's gaze dropped.

James's face suddenly grew tight with anger. "I see. Thanks, Riley," he said in a low voice. He started toward the exit.

Lord Browning hurried after him. "Where do you think you're going, James?" he demanded.

Brian, Rachel, and Dylan came up behind Riley. "What's going on?" Brian wanted to know.

"Just watch," Riley said. She had a feeling they were about to witness a scene.

James whipped around. "You didn't have faith that I could win the competition on my own, did you, Father?" he said. "So you sent her off on some wild-goose chase."

"She was in the way, James! A distraction—don't you see?" Browning pleaded.

James shook his head furiously, then turned to leave.

"You'll thank me someday for this," Browning declared.

James turned back to his father. "No. You'll *apologize* someday for this," he snapped.

"Whoa," Dylan breathed. "Harsh!"

Riley nodded. At that moment, she could almost feel sorry for Lord Browning. Almost!

"What is England's relationship with Ireland

today?" The judge's question boomed over the loudspeaker.

Riley glanced nervously at Dylan. But he looked cool and confident as he began to speak. He described the complicated relationship between Ireland and England. "England signed a historic peace agreement with Ireland in 1998—so that's good news," Dylan finished.

He stepped back from the podium. Riley nodded encouragingly at him. So far, so good!

The final round of the competition was in full swing. Riley kept her eyes on the door of the General Assembly room, but there was no sign of either Chloe or James.

She brought her attention back to the contest as the judges asked the Lakeview team to describe Britain's economy.

"England was a dominant industrial and maritime power of the nineteenth century," Brian began.

"Making London the biggest and wealthiest city in the world at that time," Rachel put in.

"Today, England's economy is the fourth largest in Western Europe," Riley continued. *Wow. Was that me?* she wondered. A surge of confidence ran through her. She added, "London is still Europe's

largest city and the business center of the conti-
nent."

From the back of the auditorium, Coach Holmes
gave Riley a big thumbs-up. He was beaming.

Even without Chloe, we might pull it off, Riley
realized. *We just might!*

Chloe stared at the Peter Pan statue in Kensington Gardens. Rain dripped off its upturned
nose.

"How could he do this to me?" she asked the
statue miserably. "Oh, James!"

"Chloe?" a voice said behind her.

Chloe whirled around. James! "I knew you
wouldn't leave me standing in the rain!" she cried,
running into his arms. He was totally soaked, but
she didn't care.

After a moment, she looked up at him. "Your
note said to meet you at Buckingham Palace, but
when you didn't show up..." she trailed off.

James smiled and grabbed her hand. "I'll explain
later. Come on. We're late!"

Chloe grinned as they ran through the puddles
toward a taxi. As they sped through the streets of
London, she looked at James. His cheeks were
flushed, and his wet hair was plastered to his face.

Prince Charming! she thought happily.

Chloe and James entered the back of the General Assembly room, soaked and breathless—just as Riley was walking to the podium for the oral essay.

Coach Holmes waved, catching Chloe's attention. "You're here!" he whispered. "You can still do the oral essay!"

"Coach, wait," Chloe said. She put her hand on his arm. She looked at her sister. Riley seemed so confident, so proud.

"It's her turn," Chloe said softly. She felt a tiny pang as she said it, but then it was gone.

"Ms. Lawrence," Ms. Watson said. "Your question: Is there a place for the British monarchy in the twenty-first century?"

Chloe watched Riley closely. She took a deep breath and began to speak.

"The royals are in big trouble with their subjects," Riley said. "They're too distant from ordinary people and their problems. There's a movement in this country to make the royals, well, less royal."

All of a sudden Riley's eyes locked with Chloe's. Chloe saw her freeze, lose her train of thought.

You can do it! Chloe urged her silently.

A slight smile crossed Riley's face. She continued. "The downside to having kings and queens and lords and ladies is believing that birthright makes you better than everybody else." Chloe grinned as Riley glanced at Lord Browning. "And it doesn't.

"So," Riley went on, "should England dump the royal family? Well, talk to the taxi driver, or the shopkeeper, and the chances are they'll bite your head off for even suggesting it." The audience laughed. Chloe saw Brian beaming proudly from the fourth row.

"Being part of a country is like being part of a family," Riley said. She looked directly at Chloe. "Just because we complain about them doesn't mean they don't have a warm place in our hearts."

Chloe felt a sudden lump in her throat. She knew what her sister was *really* talking about. And she knew Riley was right. No matter how much they argued. No matter how different they were, Chloe would always love her sister. That was a fact.

"The queen still represents Britain in a uniquely British way. And I for one would feel a little lost without her," Riley finished in a firm voice.

The audience burst into loud applause. And Chloe clapped harder than anyone.

• • •

After each team had given its oral essay, including James, Ms. Watson took the stage to read the final results of the competition.

"And the winner is...England, with three hundred forty-seven points!" she announced.

The Lakeview team burst into cheers and whoops. Coach Holmes rushed them like a linebacker, practically knocking them over. The other delegates clapped enthusiastically.

Riley pumped her fist in the air. "We did it," she cheered. "We really did it!"

A little while later, Riley was surprised to see Lord Browning walking toward her and Chloe. Then she noticed James behind his father, prodding him in the back. She hid a grin.

Lord Browning cleared his throat. "Congratulations, girls," he said. "You played a good game." He turned to Riley. "That was quite a speech you gave, young lady."

"Thank you," Riley said.

James nudged his father. Browning turned to Chloe. "And perhaps I owe *you* an apology," he admitted.

At that moment, Riley knew Chloe would have forgiven anyone for anything. She smiled. "I was thinking I owed you one myself, Lord Browning. Let's just say we've leveled the polo field—in more ways than one," she joked.

As everyone laughed and talked, Chloe approached her sister. "Riles—I'm really proud of you," she said.

Riley grinned. She knew that her sister meant it. "Right back at you, sis."

The girls hugged each other tightly.

"I'm sorry we didn't *really* win—you know, the way you wanted to," Riley said after a minute.

Chloe laughed. "*I'm* not. I couldn't have done it any better."

"You mean it?" Riley asked, surprised.

"Totally," Chloe replied. "You were great out there. *More* than great."

Riley felt warm inside. It meant so much to hear that. "Well, I learned from the best," she said.

"So did I," Chloe added. "If it weren't for you, I wouldn't have seen London. I wouldn't have gotten to know James. I wouldn't have had so much...fun." She stopped and smiled. "You know what, Riles? I think we won a lot more than a competition today."

We did, Riley thought, hugging her sister again. *We won each other.*

The Ultimate Fan's

mary-kate

Don't miss

☐ The Case Of The
Great Elephant Escape

☐ The Case Of The
Summer Camp Caper

☐ The Case Of The Surfing Secret

☐ The Case Of The Green Ghost

☐ The Case Of The
Big Scare Mountain Mystery

☐ The Case Of The
Slam Dunk Mystery

☐ The Case Of The
Rock Star's Secret

☐ The Case Of The
Cheerleading Camp Mystery

☐ The Case Of The Flying Phantom

☐ The Case Of The Creepy Castle

☐ The Case Of The Golden Slipper

☐ The Case Of The Flapper 'Napper

☐ The Case Of The High Seas Secret

☐ The Case Of The Logical I Ranch

☐ Switching Goals

☐ Our Lips Are Sealed

☐ Winning London

📖 HarperEntertainment
An Imprint of HarperCollinsPublishers
www.harpercollins.com

DUALSTAR
PUBLICATIONS

PARACHUTE

Books created and produced by Parachute Publishing, L.L.C., in cooperation with Dualstar Publications, a division of Dualstar Entertainment Group, Inc.
TWO OF A KIND TM & © 2001 Warner Bros. THE NEW ADVENTURES OF MARY-KATE AND ASHLEY and STARRING IN TM & © 2001 Dualstar Entertainment Group, Inc.

Reading Checklist

...and ashley,

...single one!

- ❏ It's a Twin Thing
- ❏ How to Flunk Your First Date
- ❏ The Sleepover Secret
- ❏ One Twin Too Many
- ❏ To Snoop or Not to Snoop?
- ❏ My Sister the Supermodel
- ❏ Two's a Crowd
- ❏ Let's Party!
- ❏ Calling All Boys
- ❏ Winner Take All
- ❏ P. S. Wish You Were Here

- ❏ The Cool Club
- ❏ War of the Wardrobes
- ❏ Bye-Bye Boyfriend
- ❏ It's Snow Problem
- ❏ Likes Me, Likes Me Not

Super Specials:

- ❏ My Mary-Kate & Ashley Diary
- ❏ Our Story
- ❏ Passport to Paris Scrapbook
- ❏ Be My Valentine
- ❏ Wall Calendar 2001

**Available wherever books are sold,
or call 1-800-331-3761 to order.**

HarperEntertainment

Outta-site!
marykateandashley.com
Register Now

The New Adventures of
MARY-KATE & ASHLEY

Collect
your own
Mary-Kate
& Ashley
photos!
Look Inside!

The Case Of The
Logical I Ranch

Check out the
Trenchcoat Twins'
NEWEST ADVENTURE!

Coming soon
wherever books
are sold!

TWO
of a kind
Diaries

First
in a Special
Two-Part
Series!

Shore
Thing

The
Diaries
of
Mary-Kate
& Ashley!

Hang out with
Mary-Kate & Ashley
. . . read their next
TWO OF A KIND book!

Jet to London
with Mary-Kate and Ashley!

Mary-Kate Olsen   Ashley Olsen

winning london

ABBEY ROAD   OXFORD ST.

winning london

All-new movie!

DUALSTAR VIDEO

Own it on video today!

outta-site!
mary-kateandashley.com

DUALSTAR VIDEO

TM & © 2001 Dualstar Entertainment Group, Inc. Distributed by Warner Home Video.